DAY & NIGHT
IN THE
SWAMP

GERARD CHESHIRE

Illustrated by
MARTIN CAMM

L HAMMOND World Atlas
Part of the Langenscheidt Publishing Group

HOW TO USE THIS BOOK

1 Read the daytime Introduction on **pages 6–7**

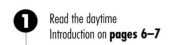

2 Open the flaps on the left- and right-hand sides of the spread to reveal **pages 8–11**, a four-page panoramic foldout of the swamp in daytime

3 Read **pages 12–19** to learn all about the daytime animals of the swamp that were introduced on pages 8–11

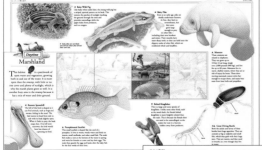

4 Check out **pages 20–21** for a handy guide to the daytime foldout. The simple numbering system will help you identify the many animals you've read about.

5 The nighttime spreads work the same way! Have fun reading!

DAY & NIGHT IN THE SWAMP

CONTENTS

DAYTIME

NIGHTTIME

▲ Swamp Trees
The trees that live in swamps need to be able to survive in ground that is damp all year round—and at times completely flooded. Their roots spread out to form a strong base, so they don't fall over.

Daytime

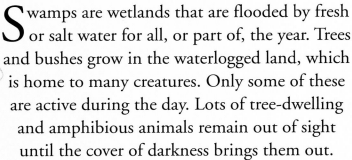

▲ Mangrove Roots
The most common plants found in swamps are mangrove trees. Their tangled underwater roots are a perfect hiding place for small fish and other animals. New mangroves grow from long seeds, which fall and spear themselves into the mud.

S wamps are wetlands that are flooded by fresh or salt water for all, or part of, the year. Trees and bushes grow in the waterlogged land, which is home to many creatures. Only some of these are active during the day. Lots of tree-dwelling and amphibious animals remain out of sight until the cover of darkness brings them out.

◄ Map
This map shows where the world's wetlands are found. Wetlands include swamps, marshes, bogs, and deltas. These habitats vary greatly according to the climate and the saltiness and acidity of the water, but they all contain waterlogged habitats.

▲ SWAMP EDGE
Alligators, crocodiles, and caimans can be active at any time of the day or night. This means that deer and other animals coming to drink need to be very careful to avoid being dragged into the water and eaten.

▲ Spoonbill
These birds are waders with sensitive bills that can feel their food as they sift through the swamp mud. The bill's spoonlike tip gives them a better chance of grasping fish and frogs that they find. Like flamingoes, their feathers are colored pink by the shellfish that they eat.

◄ Turtle
Amphibious reptiles, like turtles and terrapins, and true amphibians, such as frogs, toads, and newts are plentiful in swampy places. This is because they have evolved to perfectly suit the habitat.

➤ OPEN WATER

Since most predators patrol the shallows of the swamp edges, deep open water is the safest place for a waterbird, such as a duck. Overhead, a swallow-tailed kite soars across the water. These acrobatic fliers eat insects in mid-air, but also prey on small birds, reptiles, and amphibians.

➤ Kingfisher

Kingfishers have an advantage over herons and other wading birds because they can fish from a perch, no matter how deep the water. They take their prey by surprise, suddenly diving in without warning.

▲ HIGH GROUND

Skunks need to find areas of high ground in the swamp because they raise their young in underground burrows, called dens. It would be a disaster if these filled with water.

➤ Moth

Most of the insects found in swamps, such as this moth, use camouflage to avoid being spotted by predators.

◀ MARSHLAND

Manatees and dugongs are aquatic mammals that breathe air, just like whales and dolphins. The difference is that they are strictly vegetarian and graze on the water weeds growing in the marshy areas of the swamp. For this reason they are sometimes called water cows.

◄ Red-capped Woodpecker

This type of woodpecker is well-known for its tapping noise. Although its beak is designed for chiseling wood to find insect grubs, and to excavate nest holes, it is also used for communication. The bird makes a series of taps that echo through the forest, so that other woodpeckers know where they are.

▼ Mosquito Larva and Pupa

Mosquitoes are members of the true fly family, as they have just one pair of wings. The females are well-known for biting humans and other animals to feed on their blood, which they need to develop their eggs. The eggs are laid on the water's surface, and hatch into larvae (left) that breathe air through tubes at the end of their tails. When the larvae become pupae (below) they breathe through their "horns."

Daytime

Swamp Edge

The edge of the swamp, where the water meets the land, is called a "transitional" habitat. This is where amphibious animals enter and leave the water. It is also where waterside hunters look for their prey and where animals come to drink. This is the busiest place in the swamp.

➤ Southern Spring Peeper

The name "peeper" comes from the very loud mating call of this tiny tree frog. It grows to just 1 inch (25 mm) long, but its song carries a long way thanks to its vocal sac, which fills with air and vibrates like the sound-box of a musical instrument.

▲ Great Ramshorn Water Snail

This water snail's name refers to the shape of its shell, which looks like the spiral of a ram's horn. These snails can absorb some oxygen from the water, but they have to surface occasionally to breathe.

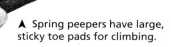

▲ Spring peepers have large, sticky toe pads for climbing.

▼ Male Wood Duck

Wood ducks are known as perching ducks because, unlike other ducks, they often perch on branches. They nest in holes up in the trees, so that their eggs are safe from predators. The newly hatched ducklings have to dive to the ground to join their parents on the water.

▲ American Alligator Hatchling

The sex of an alligator depends on the temperature at which the eggs are incubated. At temperatures between 82–86°F (28–30°C) the hatchlings will be female, while between 90–93°F (32–34°C) they will be male. Temperatures between the two result in a mix of males and females and at temperatures above or below, the eggs will not hatch.

Flexible upper jaw

◄ Baby White-tailed Deer

The tail of this deer points down most of the time, so that it is not seen, but in times of danger, it is held up (see below) so the white fur stands out. This is a warning sign to other deer and provides a marker to keep the herd together as they run to safety. The fawn, or baby deer, has spots on its coat to camouflage it when hiding from predators.

▲ Pike Top Minnow

This fish gets its name because it looks like a minnow with a pike's head. Its top jaw is flexible, so it is able to is able to grab its prey, mostly smaller fish, from below. The eyespot (or ocellus) on its tail is to fool predators into attacking the wrong end of the fish, so that it can dart away to safety.

◄ Largemouth Bass
As you might expect from its name, this fish has a very large mouth, which it uses to trap other fish so they cannot escape. In fact, it will suck in anything that moves, including ducklings and frogs. If something cannot be digested, the fish spits it out again.

➤ Striped Mud Turtle
This is a small turtle that reaches just 4 inches (10 cm) in length. It feeds on worms and other invertebrates that live in the mud at the bottom of the swamp. The shell has hinged flaps, so when the turtle is alarmed, it can withdraw its head and legs, and be completely enclosed within its shell.

Daytime
Open Water

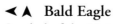

O pen water provides a range of different habitats. Some creatures live above, or just below, the surface, while others inhabit the mud and silt at the bottom. In the water itself, conditions vary depending on the depth. Less sunlight reaches the deeper water, so fewer plants and animals live here.

▼ Mosquitofish
As their name suggests, these fish specialize in eating the larvae and pupae of mosquitoes. They ar normally found in the United States and Mexico, but they have been introduced to other countries to reduce the number of mosquitoes, which spread disease. They are small fish, able to swim into shallow water to find their favorite food.

◄ ▲ Bald Eagle
Symbol of the United States, the bald eagle is mainly a fish hunter. It prefers large areas of open water, where the fish are big enough to be worth catching, as the bird has quite an appetite. Pairs of bald eagles need large territories so they can find enough food to raise their families.

◄ Swallow-tailed Kite
Like all kites, this species has a forked
tail, which can clearly be seen when
the bird is in flight. It is well adapted
to wetland habitats and is even able to
drink as it flies by skimming the
surface of the water.

▲ Tadpole Froglet
Frogs produce hundreds, or
even thousands, of tadpoles
each year. This is to make sure that
some of their young survive
into adulthood. Tadpoles are
a popular food for all kinds
of predators, from fish to
dragonfly nymphs and diving
beetles. This is why so many
tadpoles fail to become frogs.

Mosquitofish
not lay eggs, like
ost fish, but give
rth to live young.

◄ Alligator Gar
Unlike the little mosquitofish, the
alligator gar is a monster that can
grow up to 10 feet (3 m) long. It
belongs to an ancient group of
fish, called ray-fins, that have thin
bones in their fins. The alligator
gar is perfectly suited to swamps
and can survive on land for up
to two hours by breathing
air. This means it can drag
itself across higher ground
in search of fresh water.

▲ Snake-bird
Also known as darters and anhingas,
snake-birds chase and spear fish
underwater. To make this easier, their
feathers become waterlogged so they can
easily swim below the water's surface.
However, they then have to dry
themselves out to be able to fly.

◄ Baby Wild Pig
Like baby white-tailed deer, the young wild pig has a striped, spotted pattern on its back. This mimics the patches of sunlight reaching the ground through the trees and provides camouflage while the piglet hides from predators, such as cougars.

➤ Baby pike are cannibals and will eat other pike almost their own size.

Daytime

Marshland

This habitat is a patchwork of open water and vegetation, growing both in and out of the water. It is more open than the swamp, with little or no tree cover and plenty of sunlight, which is why the marsh plants grow so well. It is another busy area in the swamp because it has a mix of water and drier ground.

◄ Roseate Spoonbill
The bill of this bird is shaped so it can find animals, such as frogs and worms, hiding in the mud. The bird moves its head from side to side with its beak slightly open. When it finds its prey, the beak snaps shut. If its bill were narrower, the bird would have less chance of capturing its food.

▲ Pumpkinseed Sunfish
This small sunfish is shaped like the seed of a pumpkin. It lives in warm, weedy water and feeds on insects, small mollusks, and other small fish. The male fish makes a nest at the bottom of the water in spring and waits for females to come and lay their eggs. The male then guards the eggs and looks after the baby fish for the first weeks of their lives.

◄ Baby Pike

Even at an early age, pike are deadly underwater hunters, At first, they feed on invertebrates, but they soon grow large enough to prey on other fish— including their own brothers and sisters. Their mouths have razor-sharp teeth, so they can hold onto the slippery scales of other fish, which are swallowed whole and headfirst.

▲ Manatee

These creatures are related to elephants. They can grow up to 10 feet (3 m) long, weigh over 2,000 pounds (900 kg), and live for up to 60 years. Manatees live in warm, shallow waters, where they are at risk of injury by boats. These slow-moving mammals cannot swim fast enough to escape them, and many bear scars from boat hulls and propellers.

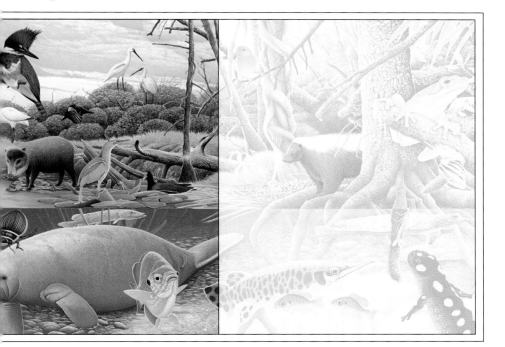

▼ Belted Kingfisher

This is a large and noisy species of kingfisher. Unlike most other birds, such as the wood duck, the female belted kingfisher is more brightly colored than the male. This is because the female does not need to be camouflaged, as she makes her nest in a burrow, hidden away from predators.

adult

larva

◄▲ Great Diving Beetle

Both the adults and larvae of these beetles have huge appetites. They eat animals as big as tadpoles and small fish, which they grab with their large jaws. They are insects, and they need to breathe air, even though they live in water.

◄ Florida Tree Snail
The shells of Florida tree snails vary according to their diets and habitats. There are about 60 different patterns, colors, and sizes, but they are always the same shape. Colors range from almost solid dark brown or plain white to bold stripes of pink, yellow, and green.

▼ Spotted Salamander
Although salamanders are amphibians, they only go into the water to breed. They spend the rest of their time living in the moist leaf litter on higher ground. Spotted salamanders prefer to breed in temporary pools of water, where predators are less likely to be lurking.

Daytime
High Ground

Between the areas of swamp and marshland are islands and strips of higher ground. Their size varies according to the rainfall—some may be completely underwater during the wet season, then reappear when the dry season returns. Many are covered by trees and shrubs, and are home to most of the mammals that live in the swamp.

▲ Gar
Gar are able to live in water where there is not enough oxygen for other fish to survive because they have lunglike air bladders and can surface to breathe. The fish's body is covered with hard, diamond-shaped scales, giving it armored protection from predators.

► Skunk
These creatures are well-known for defending themselves by squirting a foul-smelling odor from glands near the base of their tails. It is so effective that they show little fear of predators or humans. Their tame behavior makes them good pets.

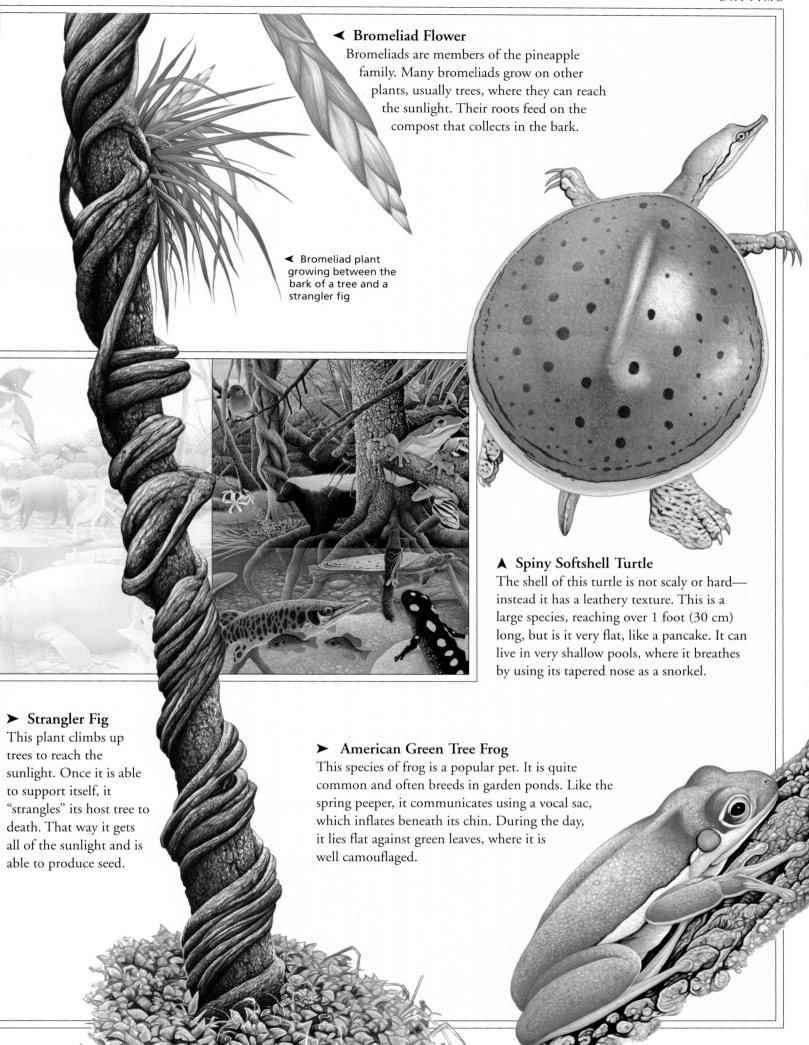

◄ **Bromeliad Flower**
Bromeliads are members of the pineapple family. Many bromeliads grow on other plants, usually trees, where they can reach the sunlight. Their roots feed on the compost that collects in the bark.

◄ Bromeliad plant growing between the bark of a tree and a strangler fig

▲ **Spiny Softshell Turtle**
The shell of this turtle is not scaly or hard—instead it has a leathery texture. This is a large species, reaching over 1 foot (30 cm) long, but is it very flat, like a pancake. It can live in very shallow pools, where it breathes by using its tapered nose as a snorkel.

➤ **Strangler Fig**
This plant climbs up trees to reach the sunlight. Once it is able to support itself, it "strangles" its host tree to death. That way it gets all of the sunlight and is able to produce seed.

➤ **American Green Tree Frog**
This species of frog is a popular pet. It is quite common and often breeds in garden ponds. Like the spring peeper, it communicates using a vocal sac, which inflates beneath its chin. During the day, it lies flat against green leaves, where it is well camouflaged.

Daytime

KEY TO FOLDOUT

Use these numbers if you want to identify any of the animals in the Daytime foldout. Most of the animals are featured on pages 12–19 and are listed here in bold type. Those that are not featured on pages 12–19 are also listed here, together with a brief description.

11 Zebra Longwing Butterflies. With a lifespan of up to six months, these are among the longest-living butterflies.

12 Double-crested Cormorants. Cormorants do not have fully waterproofed plumage, so they have to dry their feathers after fishing.

13 Eastern Tiger Swallowtail Butterfly. This beautiful insect can also be a dark blue-gray.

1 Screech Owl. These are small owls that feed mainly on invertebrates, such as insects, spiders and earthworms.

2 **Southern Spring Peeper**

3 **Wood Duck (male)**

4 **Pike Top Minnow**

5 **American Alligator**

6 **Great Ramshorn Water Snail**

7 Pygmy Backswimmer. This water bug preys on tiny invertebrates including the larvae of mosquitoes.

8 Sailfin Molly. This small fish can live in brackish water (where freshwater and seawater mix together).

9 **White-tailed Deer**

10 **Red-capped Woodpecker**

14 Great Blue Heron. This bluish-gray bird is the largest and most widespread heron in North America. It spears fish and amphibians with its sharp bill and swallows them whole.

15 **Snake-bird**

16 **Tadpoles**

17 **Mosquitofish**

18 **Largemouth Bass**

19 **Striped Mud Turtle**

20 **Alligator Gar**

21 **White-Faced Whistling Duck.** This wood duck holds itself in an upright position, so that it can keep watch for predators in tall grass.

22 **Swallow-tailed Kite**

23 **Bald Eagles**

24 **Belted Kingfisher**

28 Least Bittern. This bird is hard to spot among reeds, because it uses its posture and coloring to imitate the stalks of the reed bed.

29 **Roseate Spoonbill**

30 Purple Finch. This is one of several species of rose finches. They look as if they have been dipped headfirst in reddish ink.

36 **Spotted Salamander**

37 Peacock-eyed Bass. This little fish usually grows to 3 inches (7.5 cm), but can reach twice that size.

38 **Gar**

39 **Pumpkinseed Sunfish**

40 **Manatee**

41 **Pike**

42 **Great Diving Beetle**

25 Wood Stork. The head and neck of this bird are featherless so that they don't get clogged with mud and swamp detritus.

26 **Wild Pig**

27 Red-Winged Blackbird (male). The male bird defends its territory fiercely. Like many songbirds, the female is a dull color so she is camouflaged in the nest.

31 **American Green Tree Frog**

32 Raccoon. Raccoons are widespread in North America, where they can adapt to many different types of habitat, from swamps to backyards.

33 **Florida Tree Snail**

34 **Spiny Softshell Turtle**

35 Smoky Rubyspot Demoiselle. Large damselflies are known as demoiselles. Their larvae are aquatic predators.

43 Common Gallinule or Moorhen. This bird is found on all continents except Australasia and Antarctica.

44 **Skunk**

45 Harlequin Duck (male). This duck is a rare visitor to the swamp, preferring colder, coastal areas.

46 **Mosquito: Larva and Pupa**

47 **Strangler Fig**

48 **Bromeliads**

▼ Baby Alligator
Baby alligators eat small fish, amphibians, and invertebrates, but take larger prey as they themselves grow larger. About half of those that hatch are eaten by adult alligators during their first year of life.

Nighttime

Under cover of darkness many creatures awaken and go about their business in the swamps. Prey species have adapted to nocturnal living to avoid being eaten. The trouble is that many predator species have adapted to be active during the night, too.

▲ Bats and Moths
Bats eat many flying insects, especially beetles and moths. They use echolocation to find their prey and avoid obstacles while flying. They do this by making high-pitched squeaks that bounce off objects. The bats then pick up the echo of the squeaks to hear what's in their path.

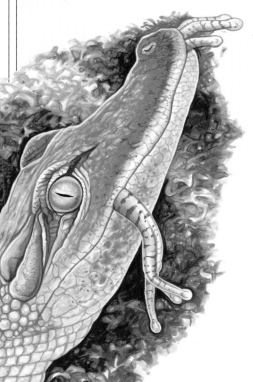

➤ Alligator
Alligators are so well designed that they have changed very little over hundreds of millions of years. They usually hunt at night because their prey is easier to catch. If they kill an animal that is too big to eat in a single bite, they will pull it into the water and leave it to rot, so that it is easier to pull apart later.

▲ WATER'S EDGE
In places where water meets land, there is always lots of activity. Animals leave or enter the water, while others come to drink. Also, insects emerge from the water, where their larvae have developed and grown.

◄ OPEN WATER
Otters and crocodiles are active predators in open water at night. Otters use their agility to outswim fish and seize them by the tail. Crocodiles are ambush hunters and will attack anything unlucky enough to come within reach of their powerful jaws.

◄ DEEP WATER

In the deepest parts of the swamp, it is always murky and dark, so life doesn't change very much between night and day. This is where bottom-dwelling creatures scavenge for scraps of food that drift down from above.

▼ SWAMP THICKET

The thicket is probably the busiest place is the swamp, because so many animals feel safe hidden among the roots and leaves in the swamp. This means that many predators find rich pickings too, so the struggle for life continues in the thicket 24 hours a day, every day.

► Roots
Some trees benefit having their roots grow in the rich, fertile mud at the bottom of swamps. It contains a rich soup of nutrients made by rotting plants and dead animals. In turn, the leaves of the trees provide food for animals.

◄ Screech Owl
A common noise in the Everglades is that of the screech owl. There are several very similar-looking species of screech owl, but their calls are quite different from one another.

➤ Bullfrog Tadpole

The tadpoles of bullfrogs feed on whatever they can find. They scavenge for food among the detritus, but as they grow larger they begin to prey on small fish and other aquatic creatures.

▼ Carp Hatchling

When a carp emerges from its egg, it has a yolk sac attached to its underside. This provides food for the hatchling for the first few days of its life.

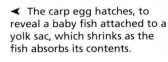

◄ The carp egg hatches, to reveal a baby fish attached to a yolk sac, which shrinks as the fish absorbs its contents.

Nighttime

Water's Edge

The area where dry land and water meet is home to both land and water dwellers. They share this habitat with semiaquatic creatures, such as salamanders and newts, that live on land but feed, or spend part of their lives, underwater.

➤ Freshwater Clam

Mollusks are well suited to life in muddy swamps because they are protected from all sides and don't need to hold onto rocks. The mud is also the source of their food, because they filter out bits carried by the water and deposited on the swamp bed.

▲ Dragonfly Nymph

The larval stage of a dragonfly is called a nymph. They live in water and have large, hinged lower lips, with teeth at the tip, which shoot out to snatch their prey—insects, tiny fish, and tadpoles. When a nymph is ready to change into an adult, it climbs up a plant stem and sheds its skin. The newly emerged dragonfly hangs upside down until its wings harden, then it takes its first flight.

▼ Walking Catfish
Many of the pools in the Everglades are seasonal, so when they dry up, animals need to find new ponds. The walking catfish uses its fins and tail to walk over damp ground in search of water.

▲ Barred Owl Chick
This type of owl has a more varied diet than most. It sometimes wades into shallow water to catch fish and terrapins. Like all owls, the chick has a huge appetite and always swallows its food whole.

➤ Cougar
Also known as the puma and the mountain lion, this large cat lives in many habitats across North and South America. It is successful because it is able to adapt to different conditions and different types of prey. It will kill and eat anything from a large deer, right down to small rodents, reptiles, fish, and insects.

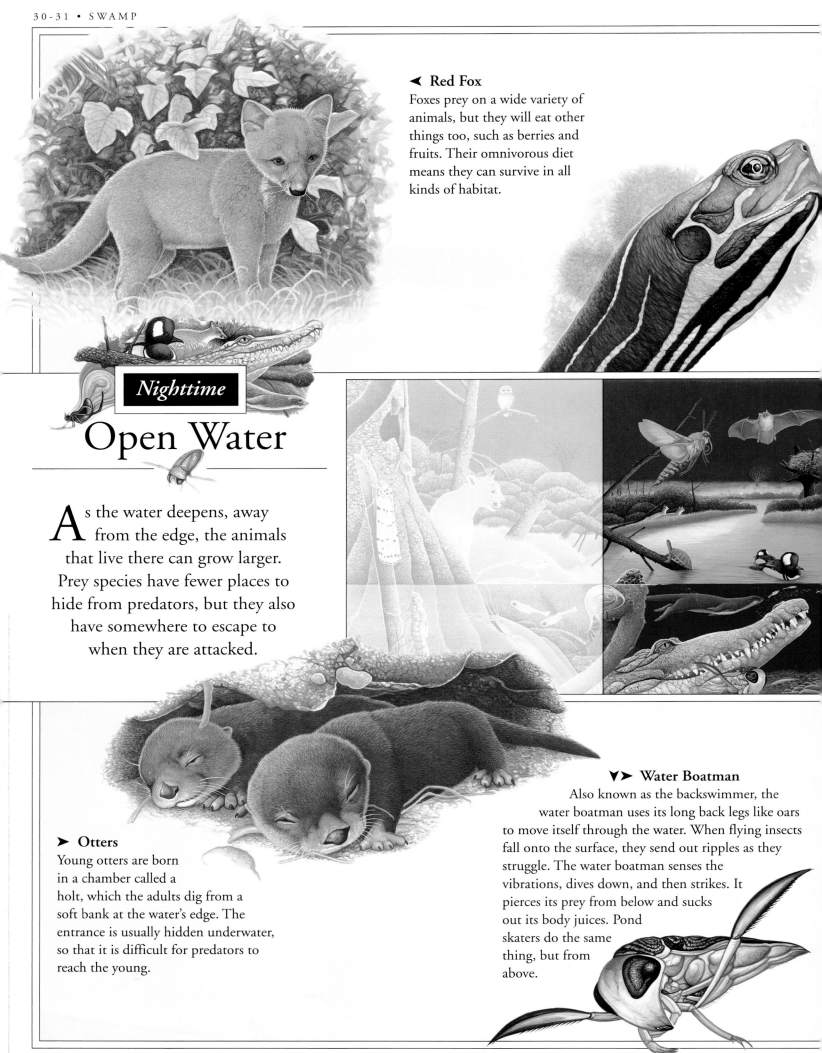

◄ Red Fox
Foxes prey on a wide variety of animals, but they will eat other things too, such as berries and fruits. Their omnivorous diet means they can survive in all kinds of habitat.

Nighttime

Open Water

As the water deepens, away from the edge, the animals that live there can grow larger. Prey species have fewer places to hide from predators, but they also have somewhere to escape to when they are attacked.

➤ Otters
Young otters are born in a chamber called a holt, which the adults dig from a soft bank at the water's edge. The entrance is usually hidden underwater, so that it is difficult for predators to reach the young.

▼➤ Water Boatman
Also known as the backswimmer, the water boatman uses its long back legs like oars to move itself through the water. When flying insects fall onto the surface, they send out ripples as they struggle. The water boatman senses the vibrations, dives down, and then strikes. It pierces its prey from below and sucks out its body juices. Pond skaters do the same thing, but from above.

◄ ► Florida Cooter Turtle

This turtle is also known as the Florida red-bellied turtle because some have a reddish color on their undersides. Young cooter turtles feed on fish, amphibians, waterborne insects, and other invertebrates. The adults switch to a largely vegetarian diet, eating water weed and algae.

▲ Water Spider

A few spiders have evolved to feed on aquatic invertebrates. However, they cannot breathe underwater, so they build "diving bells." Each diving bell is a bubble of air, held beneath the surface by a fine web of spider silk.

▼ American crocodiles eat crustaceans, fish, amphibians, other reptiles, birds, and mammals.

▲ Water boatmen are similar to beetles, but they have sucking mouthparts instead of chewing jaws.

▲ Eastern Pipistrelle Bat

The tiny eastern pipistrelle is also known as the butterfly bat because of its slow, fluttering flight. It is one of the first bats to take to the air in the evening and often hunts over water.

► American Crocodile

Crocodiles have V-shaped snouts and their fourth lower teeth stick out when their mouths are closed. Their close relation, the alligator, has a wider, U-shaped upper jaw that covers all its lower teeth. American crocodiles are found mainly in Central America. They are an endangered species in the United States and live only in the southern tip of Florida.

◄ Gray Bat
Gray bats live in caves. They like to hunt over water and eat large numbers of insects, such as mosquitoes and mayflies.

➤ Eastern Red Bat
This little bat roosts in trees during the day. It often hangs from one leg, so it looks like a dead leaf.

Nighttime

Deep Water

Fish that are active at dusk and at night hide in the deeper water during the day, where they are safe from most predators. As the sun sets, they rise to the surface to feed, then they return to the murky depths when dawn beckons.

◄ Alligator Snapping Turtle
These turtles are as dangerous as they look. They defend themselves by snapping with their muscular jaws, which are powerful enough to bite off a finger or thumb. The turtles use their sharp, parrotlike beaks to grab slippery prey in the muddy swamp.

➤ Baby Screech Owl
During the day, young owls rely on camouflage to hide from their enemies. They perch in trees without moving, keeping their large eyes shut, so they look like pieces of branch or bark.

Swamp Darter
ese fish are only a few
hes (up to 5 cm) long. They live on
bed of the swamp, where they search
bits of food in the mud. They
netimes venture up into more open
er, especially when they notice a
ce of food sinking into the depths.

▲ The roots of strangler figs and bromeliads make a good hiding place for small fish. The roots are like the bars of a cage—small fish can pass through, but larger fish cannot.

▲ Strangler Fig and Bromeliad
These two plants need trees to support them as they grow. The strangler fig wraps itself around a tree, until it forms a network of stems and is able to support itself. The bromeliad grows on branches and its roots dangle down.

Sailfin Shiner
ese are beautiful fish, often
nd in aquariums because they
so colorful. In the wild, they
to hide between roots and in
etation, where they are safe
m predators.

◄ Black Bear Cub
Black bears are smaller and more agile than brown bears. This means they can climb trees and find food at higher levels. Young bears copy their parents to discover what is edible and what is not.

➤ **Catfish (Egg and Hatchling)**

Catfish have whiskerlike growths beside their mouths. These are called barbels and enable the fish to feel its way around in murky water, where it would be impossible to see anything. Catfish are the color of mud. This makes it hard for predators to spot them in the bottom of the swamp.

◄ The membrane of the catfish egg is transparent, allowing the developing baby to be seen inside. The yolk sac remains attached beneath the young fish after the egg has hatched.

▼ **American Flag Fish**

The colors of this fish sometimes look like those of the American flag, although each fish is different. Most have a black spot on each side, which is often surrounded by a yellow or white circle. It is thought to be an eyespot, which the fish flashes at predators to scare them away.

Nighttime

Swamp Thicket

Some parts of the swamp are almost impossible to reach because of the dense tangle of roots and branches. These are good hiding places for prey animals and good hunting grounds for predators, as long as they are small and agile enough to find their way through the thicket.

◄ **Eastern Lubber Grasshopper**

When this large grasshopper is threatened it gives off a bubbly foam, accompanied by a loud hissing noise. This noise tells predators that the grasshopper is poisonous and may be deadly if it is eaten. These grasshoppers are often seen as pests because they sometimes destroy food crops.

◄ **Raccoon**

These appealing animals are very intelligent and able to adapt to different habitats and diets. In the swamp, they hunt small animals such as fish, frogs, and birds. They will also eat different fruits when they are in season.

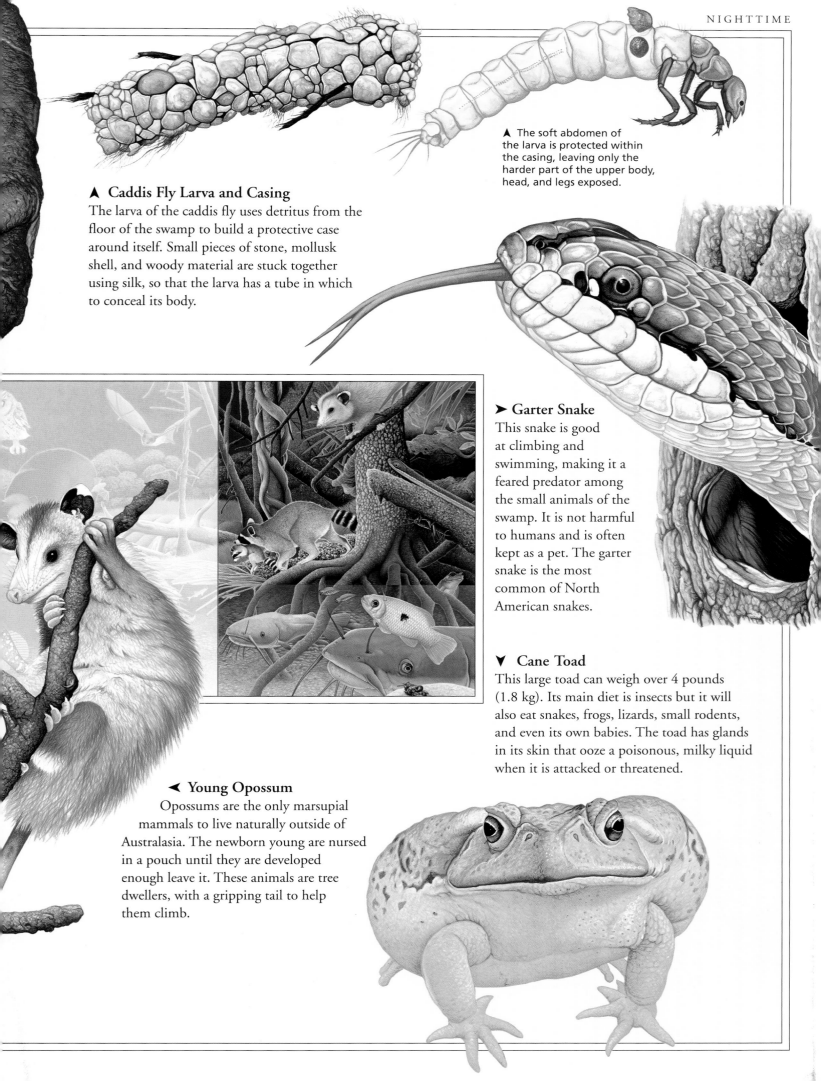

▲ The soft abdomen of the larva is protected within the casing, leaving only the harder part of the upper body, head, and legs exposed.

▲ **Caddis Fly Larva and Casing**
The larva of the caddis fly uses detritus from the floor of the swamp to build a protective case around itself. Small pieces of stone, mollusk shell, and woody material are stuck together using silk, so that the larva has a tube in which to conceal its body.

➤ **Garter Snake**
This snake is good at climbing and swimming, making it a feared predator among the small animals of the swamp. It is not harmful to humans and is often kept as a pet. The garter snake is the most common of North American snakes.

▼ **Cane Toad**
This large toad can weigh over 4 pounds (1.8 kg). Its main diet is insects but it will also eat snakes, frogs, lizards, small rodents, and even its own babies. The toad has glands in its skin that ooze a poisonous, milky liquid when it is attacked or threatened.

◀ **Young Opossum**
Opossums are the only marsupial mammals to live naturally outside of Australasia. The newborn young are nursed in a pouch until they are developed enough leave it. These animals are tree dwellers, with a gripping tail to help them climb.

Nighttime

KEY TO FOLDOUT

Use these numbers if you want to identify
any of the animals on the Nighttime foldout.
Most of the animals are featured on pages
28–35 and are listed here in bold type. Those
that are not featured on pages 28–35 are also
listed here, together with a brief description.

1 Bella Moth. This beautiful moth
appears in many colors. It rests
at night and flies during the day.

2 Evening Bat. This small bat roosts
in holes in trees and behind loose
bark.

3 **Barred Owl**

4 **Cougar**

5 **Red Foxes**

6 **Florida Cooter Turtle**

7 **Eastern Pipistrelle Bat**

8 **Screech Owl**

9 Bald Eagle (asleep). This bird is a top
predator and is found in various
habitats across North America.

10 Hooded Merganser (male)
Mergansers are unusual ducks that
have saw-toothed bills. This helps
them grip their slippery prey.

1 Black Bear
2 Eastern Red Bat
3 Gray Bat
4 Eastern Lubber Grasshopper
5 Strangler Fig
6 Opossum

22 Alligator Snapping Turtle
23 Lake Chubsucker. These fish feed by sucking in mouthfuls of mud and then swallowing any invertebrates they find.

28 American Crocodile
29 Otter
30 Walking Catfish
31 Water Spider
32 Carp Hatchling

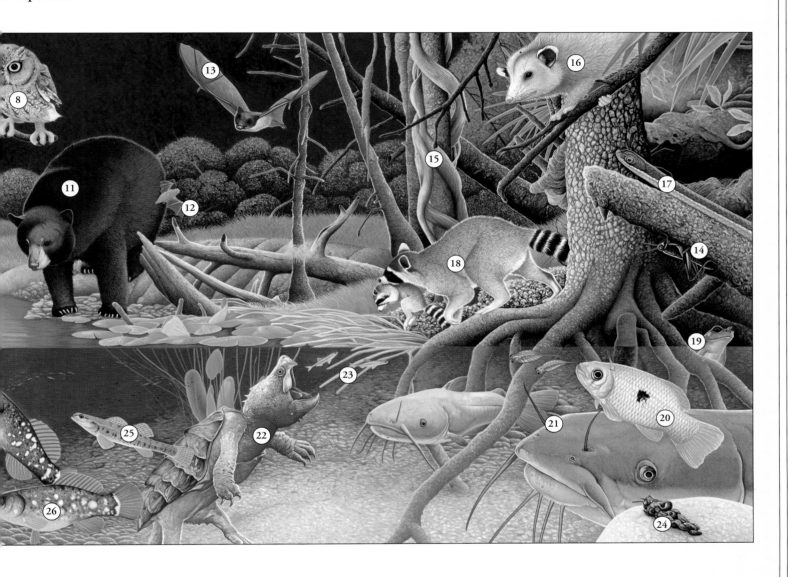

17 Garter Snake
18 Raccoon
19 Cane Toad
20 American Flag Fish
21 Brown Bullhead Catfish
This catfish is widespread throughout North America and lives in shallow, weedy, often muddy, water.

24 Caddis Fly Larva and Casing
25 Swamp Darter
26 Pygmy Sunfish. The female pygmy sunfish lays her eggs in dense vegetation and the male guards them until they hatch.
27 Water Boatman

33 Bullfrog
34 Dragonfly Nymph
35 Freshwater Clam
36 Pink-spotted Hawkmoth. This nocturnal moth drinks nectar from flowers while in flight.

GLOSSARY

amphibious living on land and in water

Australasia Australia, New Zealand, New Guinea, and neighboring islands

bog wetland with soft, rich soil

camouflage an animal's natural coloring that allows it to blend in with its surroundings

compost a mixture of decayed plant and animal matter

delta fan-shaped area where a river reaches the sea, or a lake

detritus particles of dead plants and animals

endangered a species of such small numbers that it is at risk of dying out completely

Everglades a swamp area in southern Florida

habitat the place and conditions in which a plant or animal lives

incubate keeping eggs at a certain temperature so that they hatch

invertebrates animals without a backbone, such as insects, worms, and mollusks

larva (plural **larvae**) the newly hatched, grublike form of an insect

leaf litter dead plant matter

marsh a wetland without woody vegetation, normally shallower and with less open water than a swamp

marsupial a mammal whose babies are born before they are fully developed and are carried and nursed in a pouch on the mother's belly

mollusk an invertebrate that often has a shell, including snails, clams, and mussels

nocturnal sleeping during the day and being active at night

omnivorous eating all types of food: meat, fish, plants, eggs, etc.

predator an animal that hunts other animals for food

prey an animal that is hunted for food

pupa (plural **pupae**) the stage of an insect's development between a larva and an adult

roost to rest or sleep; a place to rest or sleep

sac a hollow, flexible pouch, like a bag

scavenge search for food

thicket a dense group of bushes or trees

INDEX